Sam the Stolen Puppy

Pet Rescue Adventures:

Also by Holly Webb:

Sam the Stolen Puppy

by Holly Webb
Illustrated by Sophy Williams

For Emily Ruby,
and for Robin and William

tiger tales

5 River Road, Suite 128, Wilton, CT 06897
Published in the United States 2020
Originally published in Great Britain 2008
by the Little Tiger Group
Text copyright © 2008 Holly Webb
Illustrations copyright © 2008 Sophy Williams
Author photograph © Charlotte Knee Photography
ISBN-13: 978-1-68010-476-9
ISBN-10: 1-68010-476-4
Printed in the USA
STP/4800/0343/0620
10 9 8 7 6 5 4 3 2 1

For more insight and activities, visit us at www.tigertalesbooks.com

Contents

Chapter One
The Best Present

The living room was covered in shreds of wrapping paper, and Emily's mom was desperately trying to keep track. "Emily, was that toy car Jack just opened from Aunt May or Aunt Sue? No, hang on. Aunt Sue sent you both book gift cards, didn't she?" She stared at the list anxiously. "But I'm sure she said something about a car."

Emily's dad rustled through the paper to try and find a gift tag. "I'm sorry, but I think Jack ate it."

"Is it breakfast?" Jack had caught on to the idea of food. "I want toast!" He abandoned the car in a pile of paper and ribbon and headed for the kitchen.

"Hey! Come back here!" Dad called, a little angrily.

Jack turned back, looking confused. "But I thought breakfast…," he said in a hurt voice.

Dad picked him up and tickled him. "I'm sorry, Jack. I didn't mean to sound angry. We just need to wait a while. Emily hasn't opened all her presents yet. Come on, Emily—you're not usually so slow."

Emily was sitting quietly with a neat pile of opened presents next to her. They were nice. A pair of new sneakers. A pink fluffy winter hat and scarf. New glitter pens and a sketchpad. She *should* be happy. But she couldn't help being a tiny bit disappointed. There had only been one thing on her Christmas list.

She and Jack had both written letters to Santa Claus—well, Emily had written Jack's for him, which took forever, because he kept changing his mind, and he wanted most of the toy store in his stocking. He'd drawn a big spiky thing he said was a reindeer, and a J at the bottom, which was all he could manage, because he was only three. Dad had lit the fire in the fireplace, even though it wasn't really that cold, and they'd sent the letters flying up the chimney in a rush of flickering ashes. Emily wasn't convinced about letters magically racing to the North Pole, but it was still fun to do. And you never knew, anyway....

Still, she hadn't really expected Santa Claus to leave a puppy at the end of her bed. It had been a big hint to Mom and Dad, and they seemed to have missed it. Emily had one present left, and it certainly didn't have a dog in it. It was much too small. Though it did have very cute wrapping paper—silver, with little black pawprints scattered all over it.

"I'm sorry, Jack, I just have this one to open." Trying not to look too disappointed, Emily carefully tore the end of the package—she wanted to keep the pawprint paper. She couldn't figure out what was inside as she peered in. She'd guessed from the shape that it might be clothes, even though it felt a little hard. She shook the package, and out came something red, uncoiling itself as it came. A red dog collar, and a leash!

Emily's tummy turned over with hope and trying-not-to-get-too-excited-because-it-might-not-mean-what-she-thought-it-meant. She *did* have a beautiful toy Dalmatian dog named Georgie, who was almost life-size. Until a couple of years ago, one of her favorite games had been to pretend that he was real and tie ribbons around his neck for a leash. But she never did that now. Almost never, anyway. Mom and Dad wouldn't have bought her a real collar and leash just for Georgie, would they?

Slowly, she looked up at her parents, the collar lying in her hands, like it was something incredibly precious.

Her dad was grinning. "Can anyone hear something in the kitchen?" he asked thoughtfully. "I'm sure there's a noise. Maybe in the utility room. Sort of a barking noise...."

Emily leaped up in excitement and rushed to the kitchen door, and then through to the little room at the end where they kept the washing machine. In the corner of the room was a beautiful new basket. Emily knelt down beside it, hardly breathing, because she was so excited. The basket was padded with a soft, fleecy blanket, and snuggled into one corner of it was a ball of golden fur. As Emily watched, the puppy heaved a great sigh that seemed to go from one end of its body to the other, and then opened one eye to peer up at her. Obviously she looked interesting, because the other eye opened, too, and then the tiny dog turned around and stood up. He gave a huge yawn, showing a lot of pink tongue and some very sharp little white teeth, then padded across the basket to reach Emily. They were almost nose to nose. The puppy gave a shy little wag of his tail and licked Emily's cheek, looking at her hopefully. This looked like someone who might be good at cuddling. It had been a little bit boring tucked away in this basket.

"Oh, wow...." Very gently, Emily put out her hand for the puppy to sniff. She was desperate to pick him up, but she wasn't sure if it was okay.

Maybe the puppy would be scared.
She looked around to see Dad leaning
against the door, looking happy.

"That's really good, Emily. Taking
it slow. That's just what you need
to do." He crouched down by the
basket, too. "Pet him a little. Rub his
ears. Then when he's used to that,
you can give him a hug."

"He's really for me?" Emily whispered, hardly able to take her eyes off the puppy.

"All yours." Dad was grinning as he watched Emily's amazed face.

"He's so beautiful. Thank you so much, Dad! I didn't think you'd noticed I wanted a dog."

"It would have been hard *not* to notice," Dad said, laughing. "You certainly gave us some hints! Dogs just seemed to keep being mentioned...."

"He's a yellow Labrador, isn't he? He's so cute. You are the most beautiful dog I've ever seen," Emily told him as she tickled the puppy behind his ears with one finger. His ears felt like velvet, so soft. The puppy closed his eyes in delight. Just the right place.

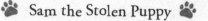

One of his back legs kicked without him meaning it to, as Emily tickled a really itchy spot.

Emily looked worriedly up at Dad. "Did I do something wrong? Why did he do that with his leg?"

"No, it's okay. Some dogs do that. My dog Scruff used to do it whenever you scratched him behind the ears. It just means they like it, and they want more scratching. Don't you? And you're right, he is a yellow Labrador," he added, reaching out to pet the puppy, too. "He's eight weeks old." He grinned down at Emily, who was still gazing in wonder at the puppy, rubbing him with one finger. "So you like him, then?"

"I love him!" Emily wanted to leap

up and hug him, but she didn't want to scare the puppy with any sudden movements.

"Good," said Dad. "Why don't you try picking him up? That's it, scoop him up gently. Make sure you're supporting his bottom so he feels comfortable."

Emily carefully snuggled the puppy into her robe, and the little dog immediately tried to climb up her front, eager to explore.

"Take him into the kitchen," Dad suggested. "Let him take a little look around. I went and picked him up late last night, and we've kept him in here since then. He needs to settle in to the house gradually. Just a room at a time. We'll keep him in here and the kitchen for now."

Emily stood up, very, very carefully, and walked slowly into the kitchen, the puppy peering around her shoulder. The little dog's bright black eyes were taking everything in.

Mom and Jack were sitting at the kitchen table, and Jack was wolfing down a big bowl of cereal. As he saw Emily walk in, his eyes went wide, and a spoonful of milk dribbled out of his mouth.

"That's a dog!" he gasped.

"Yes," Mom agreed. "He's Emily's. For Christmas. But I'm sure Emily will let you play with him, too."

Jack started to bounce up and down on his chair, laughing with excitement. "A dog! A dog a dog a dog a dog a dog a dog!"

"Be careful!" Mom reached over and moved his cereal bowl to a safe distance. "Calm down, Jack." She handed him a napkin, which he ignored entirely, still staring at the puppy.

"Why did Emily get a puppy and not me?" he asked, frowning.

"You're a little young for your own puppy, sweetheart," Mom explained. "Santa Claus brought you a remote control train."

Jack looked unconvinced. "I'd like a dog more," he muttered.

Emily sat down on the very edge of a chair with the puppy in her lap. "He's so perfect," she said. "I can't believe you really gave me a dog!" Suddenly she sat up a little straighter, clutching at the puppy to keep him from falling. "What about that TV ad?" she said worriedly. "I saw it after I wrote my Christmas letter. It said you shouldn't give dogs as presents."

Mom and Dad exchanged looks.

"It's true, Emily, it's not really the best idea," Mom said. "People often think a cute little puppy would be a wonderful present, and then when the puppy gets bigger, they don't want the work of taking care of it."

"Because it is a lot of work, Emily, you're going to need to be really responsible," Dad put in.

Emily nodded seriously. She would be super-responsible!

"But we were planning to get you a dog anyway," Mom went on. "We'd already contacted the rescue center and were waiting for the ideal puppy to come along. This little one just happened to arrive at the right time to be the perfect Christmas present."

Emily hardly ate any Christmas lunch. She kept disappearing from the table to check on the puppy. He had a little bit of turkey and some carrots, but Dad said he couldn't have any pumpkin pie.

"And Emily, you really shouldn't give him anything from the table. We don't want him learning to jump up and steal food!" Mom got up to start clearing the table. "Have you thought of a name for him yet?" she asked as she went over to the sink.

Emily looked thoughtfully at the puppy, who was having a fight with a piece of wrapping paper, rolling over with it and growling. "I think I'm going to call him Sam," she decided. "He looks like a Sam."

"That's a nice name," Dad agreed. "We don't want to be yelling, 'Here, Fluffikins!' across the park, do we?"

Emily giggled. "Actually, I think Fluffikins is a cool name, Dad. Thanks!" She knelt down next to the puppy. "You'd like to be called Fluffikins, wouldn't you?"

The puppy made a disgusted noise and spat out a small ball of wrapping paper at her.

Emily grinned. "Okay, Sam it is, then." She leaned forward, resting her chin on her hand, watching the puppy nosing around her feet, sniffing and snorting quietly to himself. Then he climbed onto her foot and looked up at her hopefully, one paw in the air. Emily giggled. "Hey, Sam," she said, reaching down to pick him up.

Sam gave a delighted sigh and firmly stamped up and down on Emily's lap until it was just right. Then he flopped down and fell fast asleep in seconds.

Emily watched his tiny body twitching as he slept. She still couldn't believe he was hers. How could anyone be so lucky?

Chapter Two
Training Sam

Christmas vacation seemed to race past even faster than usual with Sam to play with. In no time at all, Emily was back at school. She spent the first day worrying about what he might be doing, and whether he was lonely without her. When Mom and Jack came to pick her up, Emily raced ahead. Mom had to keep calling to her to slow down.

"Come on, Jack!" Emily called, irritated, as he stopped again. He was counting snails, and it took so long to get anywhere. Emily was desperate to get home and see Sam; she'd really missed him. It didn't help that Jack had spent most of the walk so far chatting away about what a fun time he'd had playing with Sam while Emily was at school. It wasn't fair. Sam was her puppy! But Emily supposed she couldn't really say Jack wasn't allowed to play with him. Actually, in a way she was glad that Jack had been there, because otherwise, Sam might have been lonely. She just hoped that Sam had missed her a little bit!

Back at the house, Sam was padding around, feeling confused. He hadn't seen Emily in such a long time. She'd been away before, but never for this long. He didn't understand about school, even though Emily had explained it all very carefully the night before and promised him that she would be back.

Sam sniffed carefully under the couch, just in case Emily was hiding there. No, just a lot of fluff and some toy bricks. He sneezed. Then he trotted out into the hallway and gazed up at the stairs. He couldn't quite manage the stairs yet, and he wondered if she was up there. But usually, if Emily was going upstairs, she took him with her.

Sam whined, and then tried a hopeful little bark. No Emily came running.

He sat down and rested his nose on the first step, tired from searching. It had been so much fun playing with the little boy, but it wasn't the same. He wanted Emily back. She was his special person.

Emily hopped around on the doorstep, waiting for Mom and Jack to catch up. Why were they taking so long? She dropped her school bag and knelt down to peer through the mail slot in the door, hoping to catch a glimpse of Sam.

"Ohhh!" There he was, flopped down next to the stairs, fast asleep.

"Emily, what are you doing?" Mom

asked as she and Jack came up the path.

"Looking at Sam. He's so cute! He's fallen asleep...."

They opened the door very quietly and crept in, shushing Jack, who wouldn't stop chattering.

Sam heard the door click shut and sprang up, barking excitedly. She was back! He was so excited that he ran around Emily in circles, jumping on all four paws and squeaking to show her how happy he was.

Emily picked him up, and he licked her all over, desperate to welcome her back.

Emily kissed the top of his head, rubbing her cheek over the soft, golden fur. "I can hardly hold him, he's wagging his tail so hard," she giggled.

"I think he might have missed you just a little bit," Mom said, with her head to one side, pretending to think about it.

Emily smiled to herself. She didn't want Sam to be sad, but it was nice to know he'd missed her, too.

It wasn't long before Sam was old enough to go out for walks. He loved it, and so did Emily. The problem was, Sam got so excited by being outside that he spent the whole time barking and yelping and jumping up and down, so that by the time they got home, he was so tired that Emily had to carry him.

"I think Sam needs some dog-training classes," Dad said as he watched Sam running in his sleep after a particularly exciting walk one weekend. He'd tied his leash in a knot around Emily's ankles, and then pulled her over when he went racing after a squirrel.

Emily nodded, but she looked a little anxious. "Will they be very difficult classes?" she asked.

"No, don't worry. I'm not suggesting we train him to jump through hoops or anything. Just the basics. How to walk nicely on the leash, sit, stay, that kind of thing."

"Ohhh." Emily brightened. That did sound very useful. Sam was so handsome, and a lot of fun to take for walks, but he wore her out, too.

Dad found out that there was a dog-training class held in the local park on Saturday mornings, which was perfect. It meant he and Emily could take Sam together. Now that she knew they wouldn't have to do anything too hard, Emily was very excited about it. She begged Mom to buy a special packet of puppy treats to take with them for when Sam did really well.

Jack was very upset that he wasn't allowed to go, even though Mom promised that he could do something special with her. He threw a huge tantrum on Saturday morning, and Emily felt a tiny bit guilty. Jack really did love Sam, too.

"I guess we could all go," she told Dad as they walked down the front path with Jack staring out of the window after them, tears still trickling down his face.

Dad shook his head. "That's sweet of you, Emily, but Jack's too young. This class is for us almost more than it is for Sam—teaching us how to teach him. We wouldn't be able to concentrate on the class if Jack was with us. He'd never stop talking!"

Emily giggled. Dad was right. Maybe she could hold a special dog-training class in the yard later and show Jack what they'd learned.

The park was very close, but Emily was feeling tired by the time they got there. Sam seemed to want to do anything except walk in a straight line. He definitely needed training!

Luckily, Lucy, the instructor, was very nice, and she figured that Sam would soon get the hang of it.

"You're starting young, which is exactly right. He's a beautiful little dog," she said, patting Sam. Lucy thought it was best for Emily to do the training, and Dad to watch and help out. "It'll be easier if he has one person in charge. Then he won't get confused," she explained.

Emily had been looking forward to telling Mom and Jack everything they'd done, but when they got home, Jack wasn't interested. "Don't want to see," he muttered when Emily tried to show him how Sam walked to heel.

Mom gave her an apologetic look. "Still grumpy," she mouthed, and sighed. "So, the class went well? Did Sam do as he was told?"

Dad and Emily exchanged an

embarrassed look. "Some of the time," Emily said. "He did stay for a little while, but he wasn't very good at the part where he was supposed to sit and look at a dog biscuit and not eat it until he was told. He had four!"

Sam sat under the kitchen table, panting to himself and showing all his teeth in a big doggy grin. He liked dog training....

Jack sulked about the dog training all weekend, but on Monday morning, he suddenly brightened. He seemed very eager for Emily to go to school and leave him alone with Sam.

Emily couldn't help wondering just what Jack was planning. It was obviously something to do with Sam. She got scolded twice by her teacher for not paying attention, and the second time, he was really annoyed. So she wasn't in a very good mood when Mom and Jack came to pick her up, and she got even grumpier when she saw Jack's smug face.

"What have you been doing?" she growled. "You'd better not have spent

all day messing around with Sam.
He's my dog!"

"Emily!" her mom said. "That's
not very nice!"

Emily stared at the ground, feeling
even more annoyed with Jack.

Jack just beamed at her. "I'm doing
dog training, too!" he announced
proudly.

"Jack's coming to dog training?"
Emily gave her mom a hurt look.
"But Dad said—"

"Not your dog training. That's
boring. My dog training. I'm teaching
Sam how to sing." And Jack danced
along the pavement, singing loudly
to himself.

Emily sighed. Jack was so silly
sometimes. "He'd have to be better

than you!" she called after her brother.

Emily and her mom expected Jack's singing lessons to last about a day, but surprisingly, he kept going. Every so often he would disappear with Sam, and he got very huffy if anyone tried to join in.

Then one Friday afternoon, when Dad got home, Jack appeared in the kitchen looking very pleased with himself.

"Me an' Sam have something to show you!" he said excitedly.

Mom and Emily exchanged a look. "Is it your singing?" Mom asked kindly.

Jack nodded. "You all have to listen. Sit down, Daddy," he ordered.

Dad had been putting the kettle on, but he grinned and found a chair.

"Go on, then. Where's the star?"

Jack opened the kitchen door and peered around. "Sam! Sammy! C'mon!"

Sam pattered in.

"Everybody shhhh!" Jack hissed. He sat down on the floor with Sam and started to sing "Row, Row, Row Your Boat."

Sam wagged his tail, lifted his nose up to the ceiling, and barked along. "Ruff, ruff, ruff-ruff-ruff...."

When they finished, with a long howl from Sam, there was a stunned silence in the kitchen.

"Did I just imagine that?" Dad asked.

Emily shook her head. "No, he really did it!" She knelt down to make a big fuss of Sam. "You're such a clever boy! I can't believe you taught him that, Jack! That's amazing!"

"We're going to learn Yankee Doodle next," Jack said, happy with the reaction he'd gotten. "But it's a little harder."

The real dog-training classes started to go a lot better after the first couple of weeks—it was as though Sam suddenly got the hang of it. Emily was really proud of him at the classes. He was so little compared to some of the other dogs, but he was one of the best ones there.

"Sam, sit!" Emily was standing just in front of him. Sam looked up at her inquiringly. Oh, yes, he knew this one. He thumped his bottom down, tail swishing the grass happily.

"Good boy! Now, stay!" Emily turned and walked away.

Sam watched her uncertainly. He wanted to follow Emily, but he knew he wasn't supposed to. He gave a little whine, hoping she might come back to him.

Emily looked around. "Stay, Sam!" she said firmly.

Sam sighed and watched Emily with his head to one side, waiting. Yes! Now she was calling him. He leaped up and raced toward her, bouncing around her legs happily.

"He's doing really well, Emily. You've worked hard with him." Lucy, the class instructor, was smiling at Sam. "You handsome boy." She tickled him under the chin, and Sam closed his eyes blissfully. "Okay, everyone, we're going to practice that a few more times."

Emily told Sam to sit again and walked back to the other side of the training area. Sam waited beautifully, and Emily glowed with pride. Quite a few people were standing with Dad, watching the class, and she imagined them all thinking how well behaved he was. One couple seemed particularly interested in the dogs, and Emily was sure she saw them point to Sam. They had a beautiful pointer with them.

Maybe they wanted to bring him to the class, although he looked a little old. As Emily watched, the pointer half-turned to look at a dog walking behind him, and the man who was holding his leash yanked him back really hard.

The dog crouched back against the man's legs with his shoulders hunched, looking miserable, and Emily gasped. That was so mean!

The man caught her watching and smiled at her. Emily looked away quickly. She'd almost forgotten Sam, and she turned back to call him.

Sam had gotten bored waiting, and he thought Emily had forgotten him, too. He was creeping very slowly toward her on his bottom, with a "please don't scold me!" look on his face.

Emily giggled. He was so funny!

Emily soon stopped thinking about the couple with the pointer—she was too busy concentrating on Sam. At the end of the class, Dad was full of praise for both of them, and they were all walking happily back to the park gates when Sam turned around and yapped. The pointer was right behind him, and he wanted to say hello.

"Oh, I'm sorry," Dad said to the man holding him. "Is your dog friendly? Sam hasn't met that many other dogs yet, and he gets a little excited."

Emily glared. That wasn't fair. Sam did like meeting other dogs, but they shouldn't have been letting their pointer get that close if they didn't want Sam to talk to him.

"Don't worry! Felix is very friendly," the man said, smiling.

Emily didn't think the pointer looked that friendly. He looked as though he was too scared of being scolded to do anything. He cowered away from the man, and something about the man's too-nice voice made Emily shiver. She didn't trust him.

"Your puppy is beautiful," the woman who was with him said. "Is he a Labrador?"

Dad said that Sam was indeed a yellow Lab and mentioned the rescue center where they'd adopted him. The couple seemed very interested and asked a lot of friendly questions, but Emily still didn't like them. She tugged at Dad's hand, hoping to get him to leave, but he ignored her.

"Da-aaad…. Can we go?" Emily muttered.

Dad looked down at her in surprise. "In a minute, Emily. We're just talking." He frowned at her in a way that said "Behave!" and Emily scowled back. Couldn't Dad see these weren't nice people?

The woman crouched down to pet
Sam, and he backed away up against
Emily and growled.

"Sam!" Dad sounded shocked, but
Emily was glad. She didn't want them
touching him!

The woman smiled. "Don't worry," she said. "I probably smell like Felix, and he doesn't like it."

Sam huddled close to Emily, still growling, but faintly so that only she could hear him. The woman didn't smell like Felix; she smelled like a lot of dogs. A lot of unhappy dogs, and he didn't want to be anywhere near her. He didn't want to end up like Felix.

Dad and Emily set off for home with Sam trotting along, walking to heel, like he'd been taught. Occasionally Emily had to remind him, but not very often.

Dad wasn't noticing how well Sam was doing, though. "Emily, that was very rude just now. You know better than that. Why were you acting like that?"

Emily shrugged. It sounded silly,

now that they'd left the strange couple behind. "They just didn't seem very nice," she muttered. "I didn't like them being so interested in Sam."

"Emily, those people were perfectly nice. Don't be so silly," Dad snapped.

"But Sam didn't like them, either!" Emily protested. "Dogs are good at telling what people are really like!"

"Sam just picked up on your bad behavior," Dad said sternly. "I don't want either of you being like that again. Now let's go home."

Emily walked along, glaring at the pavement as they turned onto their street. Dad was being unfair, she was sure. She knew she was right not to trust them.

Sam looked up at her anxiously,

sensing that something was wrong. Then suddenly the fur prickled on the back of his neck, and he looked behind him. His low growl jolted Emily out of her sulk, and she turned to see what Sam had seen.

The couple with the pointer was just walking past the end of Emily's street, watching them....

Chapter Three
Missing!

Now that Sam was walking so well on the leash, Mom let Emily take him on their walk to school on Monday morning. She said it wouldn't be every day, though, because she couldn't handle Sam and Jack!

They met several of Emily's school friends on the way, and they all fussed over Sam.

"He's so cute!" Emily's friend Ruby exclaimed, rubbing Sam behind his ears. "You're so lucky, Emily. My parents would never let me have a dog."

Emily grinned and gave Mom a quick, grateful look. She knew she was lucky. Then she stiffened, her heart jumping

in surprise. It was those people again!
The ones with Felix! Dad had said
they were the Watsons. She watched
as they walked past on the other side
of the street. Felix looked even sadder
than he had on Saturday—his head
hung low, and his tail drooped.

"What's the matter, Emily?" Mom asked curiously, watching them, too.

"N-nothing…." Emily didn't want to sound silly, especially not with Ruby there. "I just saw someone from dog training, that's all." She supposed they had every right to walk around the town. Maybe they just happened to live on a street near school, and Emily's house, and the park…. But she still had the strangest feeling that they were watching her. And Sam.

Emily tried not to worry about the man and woman with the pointer. Dad had been so sure she was being silly. But she couldn't help looking over her shoulder every so often on the walk home from school, and the drive to her ballet class.

She gave Sam an extra-big hug that night as they settled down to sleep. Mom had been a little worried about Sam sleeping on Emily's bed, but he was house-trained now, and he howled if he was left downstairs! Emily was sure she slept much better with Sam curled up on her toes, although Dad had commented that they might need to get her a bigger bed when Sam was a fully-grown dog!

Sam loved sleeping on Emily's bed, and he was sure that his basket was only for daytime naps. There was no way he was going to let Emily sleep without him guarding her.

That night, Sam was snoozing happily when his comfy nest of blankets suddenly wriggled. He opened one eye sleepily, and it wriggled again. This time he sat up and let out an indignant little woof. What was Emily doing? All he could see of her was a huddle of covers. He padded gently farther up the bed to investigate.

Emily was muttering in her sleep, hitting her pillow with her hands. Anxiously, Sam whined in her ear, trying to wake her up, but she didn't notice him. Sam looked worriedly at her for a moment. Something was obviously wrong. He stuck his cold, wet nose in the hollow under Emily's chin, knowing that would wake her.

"Oh!" Emily sat up, looking relieved and scared at the same time. She hugged Sam. "Oh, Sam, that was horrible. I was having a really weird dream about those people we saw in the park." She shuddered, and Sam licked her sympathetically. He didn't really understand what she meant, but she was obviously upset.

Emily shook her head, feeling dazed. She couldn't remember the dream clearly, just confused mind-pictures of a bunch of dogs barking sadly. But she knew it had been horrible, and she didn't want to remember any more.

Sam snuggled up against her, trying to tell her that it would be all right.

"Oh, Sam…." Sleepily, Emily lay back down. "I do love you."

Sam *did* understand that. Emily said it often, and he knew it was very important.

I love you, too, he told her firmly. *And I'll always be here. Now go to sleep.* And this time he curled up by her shoulder, determined that nothing was going to hurt her, not while he was there to take care of her.

But when Emily got home from school the next day, Sam wasn't rushing down the hallway to see her. Usually he met her at the door, barking delightedly, and wanting attention, but today there was no whirling, barking ball of golden fur. Emily checked upstairs while Mom tried to get Jack out of his coat. When she came back down, Mom had started making their dinner and was trying to explain to Jack why he couldn't have fish sticks every day, and it had to be pasta sometimes. She didn't really notice when Emily dashed out into the backyard to look for Sam.

Sam wasn't there. Emily hadn't really expected him to be—Mom wouldn't

63

have left him out in the yard while she went to pick her up from school, but she'd been getting a little desperate. Sam wasn't upstairs, and he definitely wasn't downstairs, so if he wasn't in the yard, *where was he?*

"Mom, I can't find Sam!" Emily burst out as she raced back into the kitchen.

"Don't bang the door like that, Emily!" Mom said with her head in the fridge.

"I'm sorry, but Mom, where's Sam?"

"I should think he's upstairs, taking a nap. I *think* that's where he was when we left." Mom still wasn't really paying attention. "Or in the backyard, maybe?"

"I just looked in the backyard!"

Emily grabbed her mom's arm, desperate to make her listen. "He's not upstairs either. I looked. He's not anywhere, Mom!"

"He must be…." Mom was actually paying attention now, but she didn't seem to realize how serious this was. "He probably got shut in one of the rooms by accident while I was vacuuming. Go and check all the bedrooms, Emily."

Jack looked around from the table, where he was playing with his toy diggers. "No, Mommy, Sam's with the lady," he said helpfully.

Emily and Mom turned to stare at him, and Emily gasped in horror. "What lady?" she asked, barely able to speak.

Jack just shrugged. "The one who came to borrow Sam. When you were upstairs, Mommy."

Mom knelt down by Jack's chair and tried to get him to explain, but it was hard to get him to give any more details. He'd been riding his trike in the backyard and the lady had come in through the side gate. She'd said she was just borrowing Sam and she'd bring him back later.

"What did she look like?" Emily asked. "Tell me!"

"Just a lady!" Jack was sounding a little upset and scared now. He didn't understand why Emily was so angry with him, and Mom looked so panicked. "Oh!" He remembered something helpful. "She had red

gloves," he told Emily happily. "Sam
didn't like them, and he tried to bite
them." He smiled at Emily, hoping
she'd be happy with him now, but
she was crying, and he started to cry,
too. "When is the lady bringing Sam
back?" he asked miserably. "Mommy,
when is Sam coming back?"

Emily's mom called the police. It took a while, and she kept being put through to different people, but Emily and Jack stood next to her, listening hard and trying to figure out what was happening. At last she put the phone down and called them over to sit on the couch with her.

"Emily, the policeman I was just talking to is in charge of an investigation at the moment. There's, well, they think there's a gang of what are called dog-nappers working in this area at the moment."

"Dog-nappers?" Emily hadn't ever heard the word before. Jack was just listening, wide-eyed and still teary.

Emily wouldn't talk to him, and he wanted Sam to come back, and he was miserable.

"People who take dogs that don't belong to them," Mom said slowly, putting an arm around each of them. "A number of dogs have disappeared around here recently, especially young dogs."

"But what happens to them?" Emily whispered. She was still trying to understand what was going on. Someone had stolen Sam!

Mom looked upset. She took Emily's hand. "The policeman is going to come over and ask us about what happened. We can ask him questions, too."

It should have been exciting, having a policeman coming to their house, like being part of an adventure story, *The Case of the Stolen Dogs*. But it wasn't. Emily would much rather have had Sam back and no adventure at all.

Jack was thrilled to have a real police car outside the house at first, but then the policeman wanted to ask him what had happened when Sam was taken, and he went completely shy and wouldn't say anything. Emily felt like screaming at him—she was furious that he'd just sat there on his trike while Sam got stolen, and now he wouldn't even help!

The policeman made notes about what Sam looked like and said it was good that they'd let him know quickly. "But being such a young dog, I think he's going to be easy for them to sell."

Emily looked at him, confused. "But we'll get him back before he gets sold, won't we? You'll find him."

The policeman just looked sad, and then gave a funny sort of cough.

Mom didn't say anything for a moment. Then she hugged Emily tighter.

"Emily, the police will do their best, of course, but the dog-nappers are very well organized. The gang seems to be able to make dogs just disappear."

Emily swallowed. "So—we might never get Sam back...?" Tears rolled down her face, and her nose started to run. She didn't care. She stared at the policeman, who looked so out of place in their living room. "You mean we might never see him again?"

Chapter Four
Searching for Sam

Shut away in the dark, Sam howled for Emily to come and find him. This was much worse than being left at home while they all went off to school, and play dates, and shopping. He padded anxiously around the little wire pen, sniffing the strange smells. There were other dogs here. Sam could hear them, barking and whining, angry about being closed up in their pens. He was sure that there had been at least five different dogs living in this pen before him, too. He just didn't understand why.

One thing Sam was certain of was that he should never have let that lady with the red gloves feed him dog treats. When she had opened the side gate, he had thought she was supposed to be there, especially when she had the same dog treats that Emily used for when he did well at dog training. She'd called him, and known his name, and the dog treats smelled so good—but he should have known! She didn't smell right, and then she'd grabbed his collar and hauled him out of the yard and shoved him in the trunk of that big car. Sam had barked, and tried to tell Jack to get help, but Jack had just watched, looking confused. The really scary thing was, he didn't know how to get out of this pen, or the big wooden shed where he and all the other dogs were shut in. He didn't know how he was supposed to get out and find Emily again. All he could do was call her—but how was she ever going to hear him?

Emily was finding it hard to believe that Sam had gone. She kept expecting to see him pop out from behind the couch, with his tail whirling around and around, as if it was all just a silly game.

Every evening after school, she, Mom, and Jack went out searching for Sam. Emily had used the computer to make some posters, with one of her favorite photos of Sam, and she'd put their phone number underneath.

LOST!
Sam
Yellow Labrador puppy
Please help us find him!
Tel. 555-1440

They went into all the stores on the main street and asked if they could put them up in the window. Most of the store owners were happy to help, but no one called. Emily put one up at school, too, and told everyone to keep an eye out for Sam. Some of her friends took posters to put in their windows, too.

Even with all this to do, the week seemed to drag on forever. The policeman had promised he'd be in touch if there was any news, but it had been obvious that he didn't think they'd be getting Sam back. Sam seemed to have vanished into thin air. Emily didn't care. She was not going to give up—how could she, when everywhere she looked in the house reminded her of Sam? His food bowl, his red leash, his basket. The worst thing was the Sam-shaped emptiness at the end of her bed every night.

On Saturday, Dad took Emily to dog training. He'd been a little surprised when she asked if they could go, but she explained that she wanted to warn everyone in the class to watch out for the dog-nappers, and ask them to keep an eye out for Sam, too.

It was horrible walking into the park without Sam. Dad squeezed Emily's hand as they walked through the gate, and she blinked back her tears. She wouldn't be able to talk if she started crying.

Lucy, the instructor, looked confused when she saw them. She was obviously wondering where Sam was, and that made Emily want to cry even more. But when Dad explained, she gathered the class together.

"I'm afraid Emily has some terrible news about her beautiful puppy, Sam."

Emily gulped. "Sam has been stolen," she gasped out. Her voice was wobbling, but everyone looked so sympathetic.

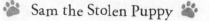

She took a deep breath and went on. "The police say there's a gang stealing dogs, so please, please don't let them get any of yours. And please keep an eye out for Sam—just in case." Then she really did start to cry.

Everyone gathered around, promising to search for Sam, and saying they were sure he'd be found. Several of the dogs licked Emily lovingly. Eventually Dad said they should go so that Lucy could get on with the class.

Just as they were walking back to the gate, Emily stopped, her heart thudding. It was that couple again! They'd been watching the class.

"What's the matter, Emily?" Dad asked gently.

"It's those people! The ones who were asking all the questions about Sam!" Emily stared at them. They had the pointer with them again, and he was plodding along with his tail drooping. *No one who really loves dogs could have a dog who was so unhappy,* Emily thought. Wasn't it suspicious that Sam had disappeared just a couple of days after those people had been so interested in him? She glared angrily at the woman, not caring if she was being rude. The woman caught her looking and said something to the man. Emily was sure she looked guilty.

Suddenly, Emily's breath caught in her throat. She tugged Dad's hand urgently. "Look! Look!" she managed to gasp.

"What is it?"

"She's wearing *red gloves*!" Emily hissed. "Don't you remember? Jack said the lady who took Sam had red gloves! It all fits. It was them! They're the dog-nappers!"

"Emily, I know you're upset, but you can't accuse someone of stealing Sam just because of her gloves." Dad sounded embarrassed. He was pretty sure the man and woman had heard what Emily said.

Emily watched furiously as the couple got closer to the gate. How could Dad not understand? It was so obvious!

The woman smiled sympathetically as they came past. "We heard some of the people from the dog-training class saying that your puppy had been stolen," she said, looking right at Emily. "I'm so sorry. He's a darling. I really hope you get him back."

The man shook his head. "I can't imagine how we'd feel if someone took Felix."

They really sounded as though they meant it. Emily just stared at the ground. She felt so confused. She'd been sure that this was the lady Jack had described, but maybe Dad was right. Was it careless to decide somebody was a dog thief, just because she had red gloves?

Chapter Five
Detective Emily

That night, it took Emily a long time to fall asleep. She sat up in bed, hugging her knees and worrying. What if it *was* the suspicious couple who'd taken Sam? It made her shudder, thinking about him being with them. They *seemed* nice—but then she'd seen them be horrible to Felix the pointer, and there was just something about them that felt wrong. Sam had definitely sensed it, too, and people said dogs always knew. Anyway, shouldn't she do something? The problem was, what? She wondered about calling the policeman, but honestly, why would he believe her? She didn't have any real proof, and she wasn't absolutely certain herself.

Eventually Emily dozed off, but she was still worrying in her sleep. She seemed to be able to hear Sam, and he was crying for her! It wasn't just Sam, either. A bunch of dogs were barking and whining and scratching to be let out of their cages. Yes, they were caged, and they were all so upset. Emily shuddered, kicking the sheets off. Those people were there again. They *had* stolen Sam; she was sure of it. Just at that moment, she woke up, gasping. She felt so scared. Without thinking, she reached down to the end of the bed to call Sam for a hug, and of course, he wasn't there. Emily sat there, shaking and crying quietly. She had to do something. She was certain now that the couple from the park were the dog-nappers. She just *knew*.

Now she had to figure out what to do about it.

Somehow, it was easier to sleep once she'd made her decision, and Emily woke up feeling much better. But she wasn't really any closer to getting Sam back. The only clue she had was that she thought the dog-napping couple must live nearby, because she'd seen them on the way to school and in the park. But how was that going to help? She couldn't wander the streets looking for them.

"I've seen them twice at dog training," Emily muttered to herself. Maybe that would be the place to find them. Then she gulped. Of course! She'd seen them at dog training because *that was where they found the dogs that they were going to steal!* It was the perfect place to find a lot of dogs and have friendly chats with their owners. Most people at dog training loved to talk about their dogs and how special they were. They wouldn't think it was odd that a nice couple with their own dog were interested. They probably went around to all different dog training classes so that people didn't make the connection.

A plan began to form in her mind. *Maybe if I went back to dog training, they'll be there, too, and I can follow them home*, Emily thought excitedly. *And if I can find out where they're keeping Sam, Mom and Dad will have to believe me!*

Lucy had a Sunday class in the

park, too, in the afternoon. Now she just had to work on Mom and Dad to let her go there. She wasn't going to admit the real reason—there was no way her parents would let her go off "bothering those nice people." She could just imagine Dad saying it. No, she would have to be a little sneaky.

It wasn't hard to sit in the corner of the couch and look as if she was moping. Emily felt a little better now that she had a plan, but she could easily drag up miserable thoughts about Sam. She could hear Mom and Dad muttering in the background. They'd noticed!

"We need to get out and get some

fresh air," she heard her dad say. He strode cheerfully over to the couch and announced in a super-bright voice, "Time for a walk, you two!"

Jack looked up from his toy cars. "Don't want to walk," he grumbled.

Dad's bouncy attitude didn't slip. "Soccer!" he half-yelled, making Jack jump. "Come on, grab the ball and grab your coats. We're going to the park!"

Emily shook her head in disbelief. How easy had *that* been? Maybe she should try being sneaky more often. Although it was a shame that they had to take Jack, too, especially a grumpy Jack who complained about being cold all the way to the park.

Actually, having Jack in tow is

probably a good thing, Emily thought to herself as she watched Dad try to coax Jack along as they kicked the ball between them in the park. Dad was having to spend so much time getting Jack not to lie down on the grass and sulk that he wasn't really watching her. "Just going to practice dribbling," she called. Gently, she kicked the ball over toward the dog-training class, pretending to be using a line of trees for markers. Jack was now jumping up and down, swinging from Dad's hand and howling.

Emily lurked behind a big chestnut tree with a fat trunk and peered around at the dog-training class. The sight of so many beautiful dogs, so many of them only puppies, made her stomach lurch, and she felt her eyes go hot with tears again. She shook herself firmly. If she wanted to get Sam back, she had to *do* something. Crying wouldn't help.

Carefully, Emily watched the class. It was a cold February day, and hardly anyone had stopped to watch. A few people were gathered at the far end—but it was hard to see…. Then someone moved, and she spotted Felix the pointer sitting sadly by the man, who was talking with another dog owner. The woman was standing next to him, wearing her red gloves, laughing at something. They were there! It couldn't be a coincidence. Emily felt her fingers curl into fists at the sight of them chatting so nicely. They were probably trying to gather information about a new dog to steal.

Suddenly, the man yanked on Felix's leash, and they started to walk away from the dog-training area, waving to the people they'd been talking to.

Emily watched in horror from behind her tree. Now what was she supposed to do? Her plan had only gone as far as getting to the park. Quickly, she looked back around the tree. Eeek! Now Dad and Jack were coming over. Jack's bottom lip was sticking out, but at least he wasn't yelling anymore.

"Emily," Dad said, still trying to be super-cheerful. "Come on, Jack! Let's see if Emily can get the ball past us!"

Emily looked over at the class in panic. The couple was heading for one of the side gates to the park now. What was she going to do? There was no way she could convince Dad to follow them, and even if she said she wanted to go home, they wouldn't use that gate.

It was time for a desperate move. Emily made a big deal of running up to the ball, faking a couple of times to get Dad and Jack in the mood, then booted it completely the wrong way over toward the gate.

"Whoops! I'm sorry!" she giggled breathlessly. "I'll get it!" She raced off after the ball, which was still rolling feebly. There was a clump of big bushes close to the gate, and Emily made a big deal of rooting around in them after the ball. Then she simply ducked through the bushes and out of the gate.

Dad was going to be angry when

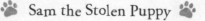

he figured out what she'd done, but right now, Emily didn't have time to think about that.

She was going to rescue Sam.

Chapter Six
Safe at Last

Emily threw a quick glance back over her shoulder as she set off out of the park. Jack was being difficult again, and Dad had his hands full. Good.

The people with the pointer were about halfway down the street, walking slowly and talking to each other. Felix was plodding along beside them, his tail drooping between his legs.

Emily had never tried to follow anyone before, and she didn't really know what to do. She was pretty sure that they would recognize her if they saw her, so she needed to keep out of sight. She jogged up to a nearby mailbox and hovered behind it, shifting from one foot to the other nervously. As soon as Felix's black-and-white tail disappeared around the corner at the end of the street, Emily raced after them, skidding to a stop just before the corner, and peering around, helpfully disguised by a large but prickly rose bush.

She kept following them, lurking behind lampposts and parked cars. Luckily, not many people were around, and when someone did walk past,

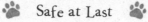

she just pretended to be tying her sneakers. It was weird. Emily felt silly hopping around behind trees, but scared at the same time. If she really was following the dog-nappers, what would happen if they noticed her? They weren't going to be happy to see her.

After about five minutes, Emily peered around the next corner and was shocked. They were gone! Her heart thumping in horror, Emily dashed onto the next street. She couldn't have lost them. This was her only chance, because once Dad caught up with her, she was going to be grounded for life.

Suddenly, she heard voices.

"Come on, you rotten dog," someone

said angrily. It sounded as though they were in one of the front yards.

Emily took a deep breath, trying to keep calm. Maybe the couple lived in one of these houses. Yes, that had to be it, because this was a long street. Unless they'd started running, they couldn't have gotten that far ahead of her.

The street was full of big, old houses, and most of them looked neglected and shabby, some with boarded-up windows, as though they were empty. The yards had high front walls, about shoulder height for Emily. She ducked down and scurried along to where she'd heard the voice coming from. It was a house on the end of a row, with a path running down the side full of old garbage. The yard was overgrown with bushes, so she peered around the gate, hardly daring to breathe in case someone heard the air hissing in and out of her mouth. It was only now that she was so close that Emily started thinking about what might happen if she got caught. The grumpy man yelling at poor Felix, who'd stopped to sniff around halfway up the path, made her realize how much she did *not* want them to know she was there. The houses nearby looked like they might be empty, with broken windows and yards that were even wilder than this one. Emily shuddered. No one was around to help her out.

At last the man and woman went inside and slammed the front door.

Emily was left crouching by the gate, feeling a little silly. She'd done it— she found where the couple lived. But what was she supposed to do now?

In the backyard, the dogs heard the slam of the front door and started to bark—wanting someone to bring them some food, wanting to go out for a run, wanting someone to pet and hug and fuss over them. Woken from a miserable sleep on the ratty old blanket that was his bed, Sam barked, too, calling Emily to come and find him. It had been at least five days since he'd seen her, but he was still sure she was going to come and find him. Almost sure, anyway.

The people who'd taken him weren't exactly cruel, but they didn't seem to like dogs very much. Sam couldn't understand why they wanted so many, when they never even stopped for a pat or a hug. The man just shoved the food bowls down twice a day, scowling, and the woman with the red gloves never came into the dogs' shed at all.

Sam missed Emily desperately. He was used to being loved, petted, and talked to. Even when Emily was at school, he had her mom and Jack. Now he had no one, and it was miserable. Surely Emily would come and find him soon!

Emily slumped down on to the pavement. "I'm so silly," she muttered to herself angrily. She felt tears burning her eyes. She'd gotten all this way, and now she didn't have a clue what to do next. She was never going to get Sam back!

But just as she was rooting in her pocket for a tissue, Emily heard barking. A lot of barking from the back of the house. There was no way that was just Felix. It sounded like five or six different dogs, and one of them had to be Sam!

Emily took a deep breath and stood up slowly. The house had an alley running down the side, and the fence looked really old and wobbly. Maybe there was a way she could get around to the backyard and find those dogs. Maybe she could even squeeze through the fence. She couldn't give up now—she was so close!

Just as she was creeping along the fence, heading for the alley, someone grabbed her shoulder. Emily froze, unable to move.

Then an irritatingly familiar voice chirped, "We found you, Emily!"

Jack!

And, more to the point, Dad. It was Dad who'd caught her, of course. Emily drew in a deep, shuddering breath and turned around. Dad was glowering down at her, the expression on his face half furious, half worried.

"Emily, what on earth are you doing?" he hissed. "You know you must never, ever go off on your own like that!" He sounded as though he was really having to hold himself back from shouting.

"Dad, please listen! I think I've found Sam!" Emily burst out. "That's why I ran off. I was following those people with the pointer. They live here."

Dad just stared at her, then at last he shook his head wearily. "Emily, how many times have Mom and I told you that those people had nothing to do with Sam being stolen? Look, I know you're desperate to find Sam, but you've just picked this silly idea out of nowhere. Now come on. We're going home."

It would have been better if he had yelled at her. Somehow, Dad's quiet, sympathetic, sad way of putting it seemed awfully right. It was just a silly idea. All her clever detective work suddenly seemed so babyish.

"Okay," Emily muttered miserably. Then she looked around. "Where's Jack?" she asked.

Dad looked down at his hand, as though he expected Jack still to be holding it. "I don't believe this," he muttered, looking around wildly.

Suddenly Emily saw a flicker of bright green through the broken fence slats—Jack's coat. He was heading down the alley that she'd been about to investigate. "He's there!" she said, racing after him before Dad could stop her.

Jack was crouched down by the fence, farther down the alley. He was listening, with his ear up against a hole in the wood.

Dad grabbed him, but Jack pulled out of his arms. "No, Daddy! I found Sam! I found him!" He jumped around and around as Dad tried to hold on to him.

"Jack, it's just a dog barking. It's not Sam." Dad was trying hard not to sound too upset, as he knew how much Jack and Emily wanted to find Sam, but he was losing patience.

"It is! Emily, it is, isn't it? You won't be upset with me now, will you?" Jack grabbed Emily's hand and tugged at her hopefully. "Listen!"

Emily crouched down by the hole in the fence. "Okay, I'll listen," she said, more to make Jack be quiet than anything else.

On the other side of the fence, Sam barked with all his strength, hurling himself against the side of his pen. It was Emily! She'd come for him at last! The miserable tone of his barking changed to delight.

"We're going home now!" Dad snapped. "This is ridiculous. What if the people who live here come out and see you upsetting their dogs?" He took both their hands and started to walk back to the street. "Emily, I'm sorry, but this has to stop. Come on."

No! They were leaving! Sam scratched against the wooden shed with his claws, fighting to get out and chase after them. How could they leave him now when they were so close?

"Dad, it really does sound like Sam," Emily said desperately, pulling back. "Please! Don't you think it could be him?"

"It IS Sam!" Jack put in. "You're not *listening* to me. I told you it was." He wrenched his hand out of Dad's and

shot back to the fence. "Just listen." He
started to sing loudly, "Row, row, row
your boat, gently down the stream....
Come on, Sam!"

And from the other side of the fence,
Sam joined in gladly, "Ruff, ruff, ruff-
ruff-ruff!"

"It is! It is him! Oh, Dad, we've found him." Emily flung her arms around her dad and hugged him, then she ran to join Jack by the fence. "Sam, it's me! We're going to get you out!" Then she hugged Jack and lifted him off the ground.

Dad was looking at the fence as though it had just exploded. "I don't believe it," he muttered. "Emily, I'm so sorry. I should have listened to you before. That has to be Sam. It just has to be." He shook his head in amazement. "Okay, well, we'd better see what we can do. We can't exactly walk up to the front door and ask for him back."

Emily looked up at him worriedly. "What are you going to do?"

Dad smiled down at her. "It's all right. We'll get him out. We just need some help, that's all. I'm going to call Mom and get her to call the policeman who was in charge of the dog-napping case. I wouldn't be surprised if those other dogs we can hear were stolen, too."

Ten minutes later, a police car pulled up outside the house, and Emily and Jack ran to meet it. "Can you get them out? Please?" Emily gasped.

"Hey, stop! You! Come back!" Dad was still standing in the alley by the fence, and he waved at the policeman. "Look, there are people climbing over the back fence!"

He was right. The dog-nappers had seen the police car arrive and were trying to get away, struggling over the fence that led into another yard.

The policeman got on his radio immediately, calling for backup to come and chase after them. "Well, they've definitely done something they don't want to be caught for," he said. "So, how did you end up here?" he asked Dad curiously.

"Emily." Dad gave a sort of resigned shrug. "She wouldn't give up, and I have to admit, she was right."

"Me, too!" Jack shouted indignantly.

"Well, we had our suspicions about these people. They've been trying to sell dogs to a pet store not far from here. But you beat us to it," the policeman said, grinning. "I've got a search warrant for this house. Know what that means?" he asked Emily.

Emily shook her head.

"It means I can go in and look around. I think we should start right about here, don't you?" he asked, walking up to the rickety old gate at one end of the fence. He picked up an old brick that was lying on the path and broke the lock. "Back in a minute," he said.

Emily could hear the barking getting louder and louder. She was sure the dogs knew they were about to be rescued. "You remember Sam, don't

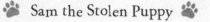

you?" she asked anxiously, pulling a photo out of her pocket. She'd been carrying it around with her all week, and it was bent and grubby, but Sam was still unmistakable.

"Don't worry," the policeman assured her. "I'll get him for you. Not that you need much help!"

Emily and Jack stood by the gate, craning their necks to see into the yard. There was a big, old shed up against the fence, and they watched as the policeman shoved the door open.

Then Emily gasped as a golden blur shot out the door, hurtling toward her. Sam!

She sat on the grass, crying and laughing at the same time as Sam jumped all over her, not knowing whether to bark or lick, and trying to do both. At last he stopped, out of breath, and just curled himself into Emily's arms, his head tucked under her chin. He sighed contentedly. He was back where he should be.

Emily hugged him tightly. It was so wonderful to breathe the sweet doggy smell of his fur and feel the warmth of him nuzzled in her arms. The strange tight feeling in her middle, all that fear that she'd never see him and hug him again, was completely gone.

Emily stood up shakily and smiled at Dad and Jack over Sam's head. "Come on. Let's take Sam home."

EXPLORE
HOLLY WEBB'S
WINTER
JOURNEYS!

WINTER JOURNEYS

THE REINDEER GIRL

by HOLLY WEBB

HOLLY WEBB

Holly Webb started out as a children's book editor, and wrote her first series for the publisher she worked for. She has been writing ever since, with more than 100 books to her name. Holly lives in England with her husband, three children, and several cats who are always nosing around when she is trying to type on her laptop.

For more information
about Holly Webb visit:

www.holly-webb.com
www.tigertalesbooks.com